This is baby Du[mbo].

Small eyes, a big nose, and ...

Ha! Ha! He has big ears!

Mommy Elephant is big.

The boys are scared. They run.

The Boss shuts Mommy Elephant in the train.

Dumbo is sad.

Where is his mommy?

Dumbo is in the circus now.
He jumps. He is scared.

Dumbo is sad, but he has a friend.

A bird gives Dumbo a magic feather.

Now Dumbo flies!

Dumbo has the magic feather!

This is the big jump.

The house is **tall**.

1, **2**, **3**! Dumbo jumps!

Ooops! Where is the feather?

Dumbo has **big**, **big**, **big** ears!
The boys, girls, moms, and dads look.
Dumbo flies!

Hooray!

Dumbo and Mommy Elephant are happy again.

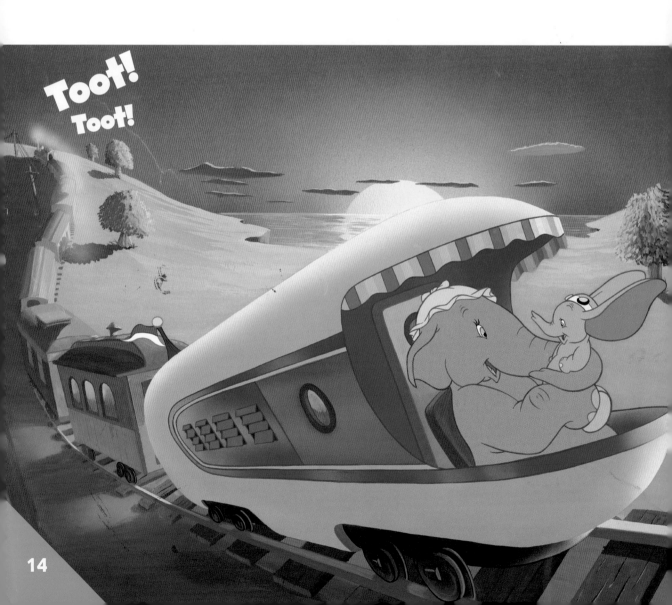

Activities

Before You Read

1 What is at the circus? Check (✓) the right answers.

After You Read

1 Put the pictures in the correct order.

2 Look and match.

Pearson Education Limited
Edinburgh Gate, Harlow,
Essex CM20 2JE, England
and Associated Companies throughout the world.

ISBN: 978-1-4082-8699-9

This edition first published by Pearson Education Ltd 2012

9 10 8

Set in 19/23pt OT Fiendstar Semibold
Printed in China
SWTC/08

Illustrated by Alan Rowe (p15 bottom)

Acknowledgements
The publisher would like to thank the following for their kind permission to reproduce their photographs:
(Key: b-bottom; c-centre; l-left; r-right; t-top)
Fotolia.com: 15 (book), c5photography 15 (cat), Eric Isselee 15 (dog)

Every effort has been made to trace the copyright holders and we apologise in
advance for any unintentional omissions. We would be pleased to insert the appropriate
acknowledgement in any subsequent edition of this publication.

For a complete list of the titles available in the Pearson English Kids Readers series, please go to
www.pearsonenglishkidsreaders.com. Alternatively, write to your local Pearson Education office or to
Pearson English Readers Marketing Department, Pearson Education, Edinburgh Gate, Harlow, Essex CM202JE, England.